Jump for Joy, Betty!

A Bugleberry Book ™

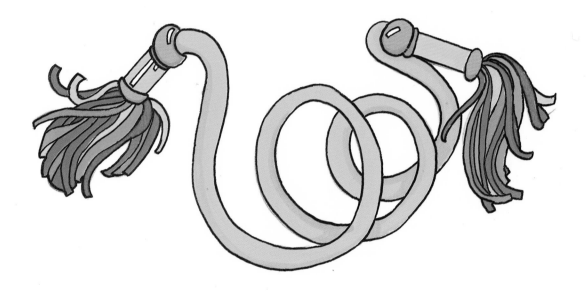

Written by Ruth Brook
Illustrated by Vala Kondo

Troll Associates

Library of Congress Cataloging in Publication Data

Brook, Ruth.
    Jump for joy, Betty.

    Summary: When Betty's friends cheerfully help her
set up a lemonade stand to earn money for a wonderful
jump rope, she realizes how lucky she is to have their
friendship.
    [1. Moneymaking projects—Fiction.   2. Friendship—
Fiction]   I. Kondo, Vala, ill.   II. Title.
PZ7.B78964Ju   1988   [E]   86-30731
ISBN 0-8167-0908-4 (lib. bdg.)
ISBN 0-8167-0909-2 (pbk.)

One day, the Bugleberries went to look at the toys in the Trumpet Toy Emporium.

There, in the middle of the store, was a beautiful jump rope. It was called a Musical Jumper. It had brightly colored streamers and handles that played pretty music when they were turned.

"What a wonderful jump rope!" said Rosie. "I wish we could buy it."

"It's too expensive," said Skip. "We don't have enough money."

6

"Well, I know how *I* can get the money for the Musical Jumper," said Betty. "I'll make lemonade and sell it. With the money I earn, I can buy the jump rope."

"I make *great* lemonade," said Dolly. "I'll help you."

"We'll all help," said Toony.

"No!" Betty cried. "I don't need any help. I can do it all myself. Besides," she said, pointing to all the Bugleberries, "if I let *you* use the jump rope, it will get all messed up!"

The Bugleberries just stared as Betty walked away.

Early the next day, Betty sat outside on
her front lawn. She painted a sign that said
ICE COLD LEMONADE—25¢ A CUP.
Then, she leaned the sign against a great big
tree.

Betty was pulling a table out onto the
sidewalk when the Bugleberries walked by.

"I'll help you with that," said Bo.

"No, thank you," said Betty. "I can do it
myself."

The Bugleberries watched while Betty
worked. Then they went off to play at
Woodwind Lake, leaving Betty behind.

8

Betty rushed to the kitchen to make lemonade. First, she squeezed the lemons and put the lemon juice into a big pitcher. Next, she added lots and lots of sugar. Then, she filled the pitcher with water.

At last, she was ready to carry the lemonade outside. But the pitcher was so full that some of the lemonade spilled onto the floor!

9

Quickly, Betty set down the pitcher and ran to get a mop. Bitty ran with her. But Betty was in such a hurry, she did not see Bitty.

SWOOSH! Betty tripped over Bitty and slipped on the cold wet floor. CRASH! Betty fell against the table. Down came the lemons and sugar and spoons and cups. The whole floor was a sticky mess!

"Oh, no!" cried Betty. "It will take forever to clean this up!"

At last, Betty went outside with the
pitcher and cups and napkins.

A long line of people were waiting in
front of the lemonade stand.

Betty set the tray on the table and poured
a drink for the man at the head of the line.
He gave Betty a quarter and took a sip.

12

"This drink is too sweet!" he yelled.
"And it isn't cold enough. I want my money
back!"

"Look, Mommy!" shouted a little boy.
"That lemonade is full of seeds!"

"I'm sorry," Betty said, "but I've never
made lemonade before. I'll get some more
ice and lemon juice."

Betty ran back to the kitchen. She took some ice cubes out of the freezer and put them in a bucket. Next, she squeezed some lemons and picked the seeds out of the juice. Then she poured the fresh lemonade into the pitcher.

When everything was ready, Betty reached into the ice bucket for some ice.

"It's all melted!" she cried. "Now I have to get more ice!"

Betty was getting very tired.

14

By the time she brought out the fresh lemonade, all the people were gone.

Paper cups and napkins were scattered all over the ground, and the sign had fallen over.

Betty was sad—she hadn't sold a single cup of lemonade! She sat down under the tree and started to cry.

15

Just then, the Bugleberries passed by.
They saw Betty crying.

"What's wrong?" asked Jingle.

"Everything!" said Betty. "I worked all
day, and I didn't sell any lemonade at all."

Betty told her friends all that had
happened.

"I guess you could have used some help
after all," said Skip.

Betty looked at her friends. "I guess so,"
she whispered.

16

The next day, everyone
came to Betty's house.
"Bugleberries to the rescue!"
they called. Then they all
got to work.

Bo nailed the sign to the tree. Jingle set
up the table. Rosie folded the paper
napkins, and Toony put stones on them so
that they wouldn't blow away.

18

Dolly measured out
the right amount of
lemons and sugar for
the lemonade. Skip
poured the lemonade through a strainer,
and Betty added ice.

Soon everything was ready.

19

It was a very hot day. Many people were happy to buy cool, refreshing lemonade.

Betty served, Skip collected the money, and Baby dropped the coins into an empty mayonnaise jar. Bo made sure that the used cups and napkins were thrown into the trash basket.

More and more people came and bought more and more lemonade.

By the end of the day, the mayonnaise jar
was filled with quarters.

"I wonder how much money we earned,"
said Betty.

Skip emptied the coins out of the jar.
They counted the money. There were forty
quarters.

"That's exactly ten dollars," said Skip.

"That's enough to buy the jump rope,"
said Betty. "I'll buy it tomorrow."

In the morning, while the others went to the playground, Betty ran to the Trumpet Toy Emporium.

Betty handed her jar filled with coins to the saleswoman. Together, they counted the money.

Betty held her breath as one of the Musical Jumpers was taken down from the shelf and packed in a plastic bag.

"It's a beautiful jump rope," said the saleswoman as she handed it to Betty. "I hope you enjoy it!"

Betty took the package and ran all the way home.

As soon as she was home, Betty unwrapped her beautiful jump rope and started to jump. The handles made such pretty music! She wished that her friends were there to hear it. Betty jumped and jumped.

Then suddenly she stopped. She had a funny feeling in her stomach. Betty missed her friends. She thought of how much more fun it would be if they could all jump and play together. And she knew how much they had helped her.

Betty put the jump rope back in the bag and went to find her friends.

26

When she saw the Bugleberries on the
playground, Betty rushed over to them.
They gathered around her and watched as
she took the Musical Jumper out of the
bag.

Betty held it out to them.

28

"Will you jump with me?" she asked.
"It's no fun playing all alone."
"Hooray!" they shouted.

What fun they had together!
The bright streamers rippled in the breeze,
and the handles played the happiest tunes.
Everyone had a chance to turn the rope
and to make up a rhyme as they jumped.

When it was Rosie's turn, she jumped and sang:

Roses are red.
Violets are blue.
Betty, we're happy
To jump with you.

31

Then it was Betty's turn. She skipped over the rope and sang:

> *Roses are red.*
> *Violets are blue.*
> *I'm very lucky*
> *To have friends like you!*

And when Betty jumped, she jumped for joy!